Ketty and the Supreme Dream Detective Team

VS. SOCK TROLLS

By Kenneth A. Flowers Jr.

AuthorHouse™
1663 Liberty Drive
Bloomington, IN 47403
www.authorhouse.com
Phone: 1 (800) 839-8640

Published by AuthorHouse 11/22/2019

ISBN: 978-1-7283-1668-0 (sc)
ISBN: 978-1-7283-1670-3 (hc)
ISBN: 978-1-7283-1669-7 (e)

Library of Congress Control Number: 2019908342

Print information available on the last page.

authorHOUSE®

This one is for My Mom Floretta Dessau.
Who never got to see her son's book
On earth, but now sees it from Heaven.

KETTY AND THE SUPREME DREAM DETECTIVE TEAM

VERSUS

SOCK TROLLS

The morning was calm. The clouds milky white,and the sky royal **BLUE**. I the amazing Ketzia, was sleeping soundly in my bed, dreaming of horses mighty and **TRUE!**

When all of a sudden I sprang up wide **AWAKE**! I heard a sound that made the whole house **SHAKE**! It was bid D, my fave name for him. His voice was loud and he sounded like he was in **PAIN**. I ran towards the sound of his voice and heard..."This is **INSANE**!

Everytime my clothes get washed something always goes missing. It is always the same thing. Never any other kind of clothing. Not a shoe, not a **SHIRT**, not a tie, not a **SKIRT**. Not a hat, nor **FROCKS**. But what always seems to go missing is one of

my **SOCKS**!" "Your socks" Mom asked. "Not socks." He snipply replied. "My sock." "Your sock?" I whispered but still loud enough for my parents to **HEAR**.Yes Ketty, my sock. Come in i'll make it **CLEAR**.

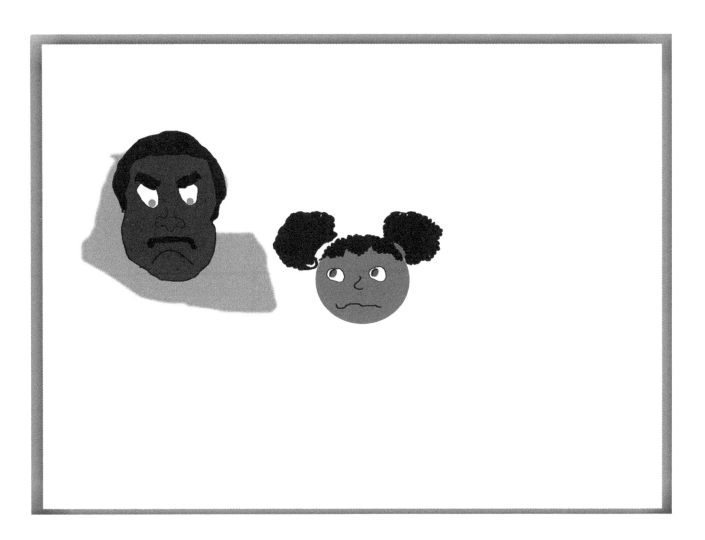

Everytime we go to the wash we throw it in the **MACHINE**. I use a sock baag for them when its time to **CLEAN**. But it seems everytime I wash my socks, one of the pair ends up missing!" "What do you mean missing?!" "Just what I said sweet pea. Different colors, different sizes, whether thick or **THIN**. No matter what I do, I can't seem to **WIN!**"

"Oh honey," Mom said. "I don't know what to tell you. I put them in the sock bag like you asked. All the colors, different sizes, both thick and **THIN**. Every sock washed with colors sharp as a **FIN**!" "You sure you put them all together? Perhaps they were not all in the same bag."

Dad shook his head in protest, waving his hands. "No snugglebug! I am sure every pair went together but only one of each came **OUT!** He looked like a baby as he began to **POUT**.

"Honey, why would I hide your **SOCKS**? Even though they should be sunk in the sea with **ROCKS**!" Mom smiled again, even chuckled a **LITTLE**.

Ketty began to laugh, her voice as high as a **FIDDLE!** "Girls", Big D said with frustration in his **TONE**. "This is not the time for laugher, but concern should be **SHOWN**." His face displayed a fake **FROWN**.

"Mom, what do you think really happened to Big D's socks?" "Don't you mean his sock?", bumping her shoulder into her daughter's. Ketty rolled her eyes. "Moooooom!"

Isn't it strange that his socks are missing? He always puts all the pairs together. But one always seems to disappear into thin air! Like magic." "That is a bit strange," Mom replied. "But what can we do Ketty? If the socks are gone, they're gone!"

"We can't go to the police and write a report about missing socks?" "That's true." Ketty said. She placed her hand on her chin. She snapped her fingers as a fantastic idea lit up her head.

"I know mom. I will do an investigation." Mom gave her a puzzled look. "An investigation?" "Yes! I will be the detective and get Jacob and Liyah to help me?"

"Ketty, getting your friends together to find out what happened to your father's socks sounds like a lot of work? You sure you want to do this? More importantly, will your friends even want to do this?"

"Why wouldn't they want to do this? This is what we live for! A real live mystery is afoot! Calling all detectives, sleuths, Scooby Doo watchers, We've got a job to do? Besides, Mom, you're missing the point." Mom folded her arms with an amused look painted on her face. "Oh am I? What point would that be my little Nancy Drew?" Ketty's mouth dropped open as she spoke.

So much Funnnnnn!

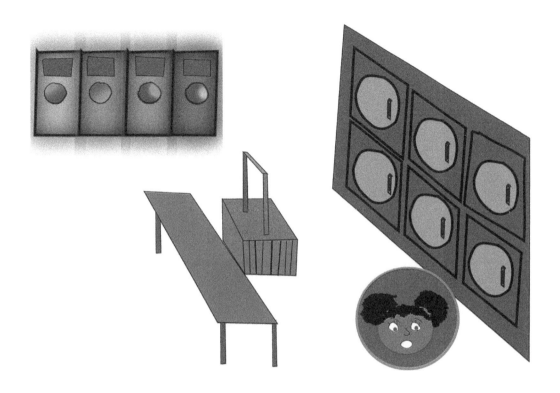

Ketty and her Mom went to the laundry mat. It was huge. It had at least fifty washing machines and fifty dryers. Also, there were loads of people with their children in the laundry mat that day. Well of course it was. Saturday was the busiest day of the week for laundry mats. Ketty sighed a big breath of air. "Mom this is going to be harder than I thought!" "Well sweetie pie, lets go to the lost and found first and look there. Perhaps we will run upon some luck!" If the lost and found is anything like the rest of the building, I doubt It", she muttered.

As Ketty and her mom walked towards the lost and found. Ketty spied out her friend Liyah from the corner of her eye. She called out her name. "Liyah?" she cried with a loud voice. Liyah lifted up her head and saw Ketty. "Ketty Ket!" she screamed as she ran to her.

They hugged each other. "What are you doing here?" they asked each other at the same time. They laughed, holding hands. "I'm here to solve a mystery, and I am so glad you're here because

I was going to put the call out for the crew to help me with it."
"Mystery?" Liyah repeated. "What mystery Ketty Ket? What's going on?"

"Why the mystery of the missing socks." Ketty answered. "There is something fishy going on here Liyah." Ketty whispered to her. Liyah had a look on her face like she smelled something fishy. "Mystery of the missing socks? Ketty we are in a laundry mat. Clothes are left in the washing machines or in the dryers or on the floor all the time!" "I know that Liyah. But I didn't say clothes, I said missing socks. My dad's socks have gone missing for the last two months! From thick to thin, every kind of colors, every sock he has. Instead of having two of each making a pair, he only now had"- "One of each!" Liyah finished.

"Yeah Liyah, how did you know?"

"My dad has had the same thing happen to him! I though it was strange. To me dad was just misplacing his socks, but he never misplaces anything!"

"Hmmmm" They both said at the same time with one hand on their chin and Ketty scratching her **HEAD**. "I got it" said Ketty. This question through the laundry mat, we've got to **SPREAD**!" "What is that?" asked Liyah there is a mystery afoot." "Don't you mean a foot with no socks?" Ketzia groaned.

"Hey

Just then voice they both knew sounded out in the laundry mat. Hey girls what's up?" They turned and saw one of their best friend Jacob. "Jacob" they both exclaimed. They all hugged. "Its good to see you Jakes!" Ketty said. "You to Ketty.", Jacob replied. "What are you girls up too?"

irls! What's Up?"

"We are sock deep into a mystery Jakes," Said Liyah. Jacob gave a confused **LOOK** "Don't you mean knee deep?" Ketty groaned and her head she **SHOOK**. "Don't mind Liyah or her bad jokes, but yes we are in the midst of a mystery. "The case of the missing socks!" She shouted as she lifted her hands into the **AIR!**

Again Jacob gave them a look as if their minds weren't all **THERE**. "Missing socks?" he echoed. What are you girls talking **ABOUT**?" The missing socks!" they said with a **SHOUT**. "My dad's socks have been **DISAPPERING**." Jacob saw her face, and the frown she was **WEARING**! "Did you check his stuff?" "Of course we did, but found one of **EACH**. We checked everywhere, except the **BEACH**."

"Wouldn't they be on his **SHELF**?" "No Jacob, haven I been talking to **MYSELF**?"

"Perhaps under his bed, or in his **SHOES**?"

"No!" they said again.

"Well how many pairs of socks did your dad **LOSE?**" Ketty sighed. "**NONE.** He didn't lose a *pair* of socks, no not **ONE.** What he lost was one sock out of each **PAIR.** Now he has no matches to **WEAR.**"

Jacob eyed them both. "Just to be **CLEAR,** your father lost his socks, and you think you'll find them **HERE?**" Ketty nodded, "this is were we wash clothes all the **TIME.** Using dozens of quarters, loads of **DIMES.**

"Will you help?" Jacob smiled. Ketty said, "Let's all spread all over the laundry mat. Liyah go left, Jakes handle the **RIGHT**. This case is going to need good ears and **SIGHT**." "Cool!" said Liyah as Jacob gave her the thumbs **UP**. Smiling like he was playing with his **PUP**. They took off in different **DIRECTIONS**.

She only found a shirt that read the name **MABLE**. They scoured bathrooms and machines that dispensed **CANDY**. Ketty thought to herself this isn't so **DANDY**! While walking back to her mom,

Combing every bit of laundry mat's **SECTIONS**. They looked in every corner, every crevice and **MACHINE**. All the while being silent, hoping not to make a **SCENE**. They looked in side washers, driers Liyah looked under a **TABLE**.

A lady with black hair folding her **CLOTHES**, left her basket near washers that stood in **ROWS**. She dropped wet socks in the basket with the sound of a **PLOP**. Some laid in the basket, some laid on the **TOP**. All different colors, at least thirty **PAIR**. There was a set of pretty blue ones, that suddenly weren't **THERE**!" Ketty rubbed her eyes, she must have been seeing **THINGS**, then it happened again, black ones with red **RINGS**. "No way" she said to herself

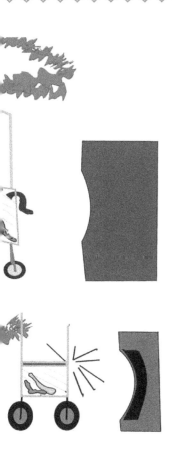

as she moved **NEAR**. There must be a reason, no need to **FEAR**." As Ketty got closer, she let out a small **CRY**, because zip the pink socks were gone in a blink of an **EYE**! She looked and smiled at the lady whose hair is long and **BLACK**. Ketty eyed the washer when she heard... "This is **WACK**!" Ketzia looked at Liyah and put her finger to her **LIPS**. Liyah nodded, her heart doing **FLIPS**.

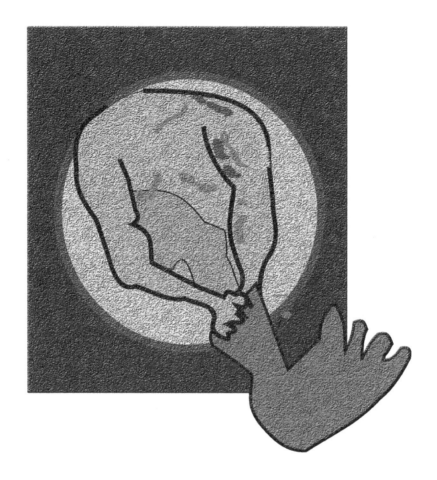

Ketty pointed towards the washer with the open **DOOR**. They stepped quietly so no noise was heard on the **FLOOR**. They heard rustling, bustling, grunting and **GROANING**. They peaked inside, as they heard some **MOANING**. They were scared of all the **NOISE**, but what they saw, made them lose their **POISE**. Inside the washer, there were pale yellow **ARMS**, putting a sock on a foot that smelled like ten **FARMS**.

Liyah screamed, the grunting stopped, the foot became **STILL**. And down Ketty's back, there came a **CHILL**. But somewhere in her heart a boldness **AROSE**. She reached in the washer and grabbed the sock with the strength of **HEROES**!

"Liyah", Ketty cried, "give it all you've **GOT**!" But the thing was strong and the washer was **HOT**. Back and forth Ketty went in and **OUT**. Ketty said, boy Your a stubborn **lout**!" Her body felt terribly **SORE**, being involved is the tug of **WAR**. This made her shout, "Give me that sock you smelly bad **THING**. It's justice to you we're determined to **BRING**. Only a snort with smoke was the thing's **REPLY**, "Pull harder Liyah, its do or **DIE**!" "I am Ketty but that thing is **STRONG**. That's when Jacob quickly came **ALONG**. He saw what was happening and joined the **FRAY**. While pulling on Ketty he said, "We're going to save the **DAY**. With that statement, all three of them became **BOLDER**.

Until one strong jerk yanked them into a place much **COLDER**. In the washer they saw a bright light, and heard a **SOUND**. That's when they began to spin like a merry go **ROUND**. We're in the washer, Jacob said, "No kidding?" the girls **SCREAMED**. Then the spinning stopped. They prayed it was just a **DREAM**. They shook their heads, looked around and saw a strange **LAND**. The detectives were amazed and began to **UNDERSTAND**.

That through the washer through detergent and **FOAM**. They came into a world on their own they'd NEVER **roam.** "Where are we?" asked Liyah. "I don't know." Ketty **REPLIED**. Then a laugh that sounded out, like chicken being **FRIED**. "Where are you?" it **SPOKE**, the team saw a shadow, but didn't see the **BLOKE**. "Where are you?" it asked as the detectives held their **BREATH**. The creepy voice seemed to be on their right and **LEFT**.

"Your mine little **NUGGETS**. If I were you, I would be crying **BUCKETS**. From my land, there's no **ESCAPE**, so by coming here, you've sealed your **FATE**." Finally, they saw something so big and **STRONG**. It was a creature at least 10 feet **LONG**. His body was muscle and fat, gleaming in the **SUN**. His skin was the color of steak well **DONE**. His eyes were big and brown, his nose was **SWOLLEN**, and his smile by a thief looked like it had been **STOLEN**. "How nice of you nuggets, to come into my **WORLD**. Me and my gang love tasty little boys and **GIRLS**." "Uh guys," Jacob said, "that's our cue to **RUN**," But Ketty stood still looking at the creature that weighed a **TON**. Her eyes went to the top of head, down to his hideous **FEET**. In her heart she thought we are dead **MEAT**.

He had a mohawk, on his arm, a tattoo that said I love **SOCKS**. On his left leg was another one that said, I like to **BOX**. On his left foot was the sock, nothing on the **RIGHT**. The friends looked at his foot and it gave them a **FRIGHT**. His foot had boils and sores, with toe nails **INGROWN**. Ketty swore that in parts of his skin, she could see **BONE**.

"I see why you steal socks," she said with **DISGUST**. He showed his teeth, which had the color of **RUST**! A crooked smile on his fade began to **SPREAD**, and the hearts of the team, filled with **DREAD**! The creature took one giant step towards them and **SAID**. That's right tasty nuggets, I steal **SOCKS**. My friends and I found doors with **LOCKS**.

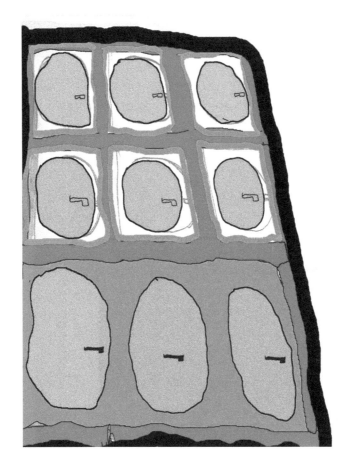

The doors lead into your world." He lifted his hands in the **AIR**. Bright lights came on, as the team just **STARED**. From left to right up to thirty feet **TALL**, washing machines and dryers were stacked on every **WALL**. Washer after washer, some looked worn, other shiny and **NEW**. Ketty and the team had just found a major **CLUE**! "What are these?" asked Liyah. "Washers." Said Jakes. "We know that Jacob," said Ketty. "The better question is who are you?" The creature **GRUNTED**, and looked as if he was **INSULTED**.

I am Org, ruler of this **LAND**. built on strong **SAND**. Master of mammals, the titan of treasures, taker of **TOLLS**, but most important, I am the king of the sock **TROLLS**. "SOCK TROLLS!" the team said **TOGETHER**. Yes said the troll, his voice rough and **WEATHERED**. "Washers and dryers are gateways to your **WORLD**. We arrive in your place, with a spin and a **TWIRL**. He glared at the detectives, with a snarl and a **GRIN**. Jacob eyes wide began to rub his **CHIN**. "Sock trolls huh? But why do you need **SOCKS?** Your feet look tough enough to smash **ROCKS**!

THE KING TROLL Org gave Jacob a face filled with mock **HURT**. He put a hand on his heart, and scratched under his **SHIRT**. "Our feet our sensitive to the **TOUCH**. Without covering on our feet, the bois and sores hurt so **MUCH**!"

"Well, Liyah said, why not buy **SHOES**?"

"Shoes?" Org growled. "Wearing **SHOES**, would give us the **BLUES**. Plus are feet in shoes would create much **DUST**. Would create really bad smells, and our boils would **BUST**. It would also create wicked funky **MOLD**. And cause our feet to turn the color of **GOLD**.

Ketty then said so because **SHOES** would bring **BLUES**, and though your feet are **TOUGH** Because of the sores, walking barefoot would be **ROUGH**, you steal people's socks and other **STUFF**?!" Org grunted as if he was **OFFENDED**. "We only take socks, nothing else **INTENDED**." "But why?", the team asked as **ONE**. More sock trolls showed up saying, this could be **FUN.** "Why? Our fabric is too hard, we only use it for **CLOTHES**. Trying to use for shoes, would add to our **WOES**. Besides it would smell up our **NOSES**. To wipe out that stink, we don't have enough water **HOSES**. So socks are the only answer, socks are the **KEY**." The other trolls joined in the chorus, with frightening **GLEE**! "socks, socks, socks, they are the **KEY**!" They inched closer to the team, who was ready to **FLEE**! "Socks, socks, socks, is what we **NEED**!' Their eyes wide with hunger and **GREED**. The sock trolls weren't even being **DISCREET**, Cause with those wide eyes, they eyed the team's **FEET**!" "We are going to take your socks" Org **SNARLED**, "because pretty socks we need for feet that are **GNARLED**.

The sock trolls began to move a little **CLOSER**. The children moved back and bumped into a **ROASTER**! Looking left to right trying to find a way **OUT**. Jacob spoke his voice filled with **DOUBT**. "We have a plan that will help us **WIN**. Org gave a robust laugh as the trolls joined **IN.** "Yes little nuggets, tell us your **PLAN**.

On the front of the bag in particular, was a red **HEART**. And in Ketty's mind, a plan began to **START**. The heart on the bag gave Ketty a **CLUE**, It was the same heart as Org's left arm **TATTOO**! Above each bag was a set of **KEYS**. This was her moment, she had to **SEIZE**. She then remembered she had laundry detergent in her **BAG**. And in her mind the plan didn't **LAG**. "Guys get ready" her voice so strong, she pulled the **DETERGENT**, out of her

bag and yelled..."Sock trolls, this is **URGENT**." "Don't come any closer, do not come **NEAR**! for in my hand what all sock trolls **FEAR**!" "Hah" Org said. "and what is that?" Ketzia hesitated, "Its my weapon I have when things go **WRONG**, it is my...sock troll **BEGONE**!" The trolls took a breath with their eyes wide with **FEAR**, they believed Ketty's words that was **CLEAR**!

"sock Trolls will DR

"What happens little nugget? What happens when we turn **RED?**" "A weird smile across your face will **SPREAD**." "And then?" The sock trolls cried. "Your tongues will become thick as **BREAD**. And..." "And then?" they cried even louder. Ketty's smile got even wider. "Your skin will turn **RED**, then your skin will SHED, and your tongue will become as thick as **BREAD**. "And then the sock trolls said again." "Ketzia whispered, looking at Liyah and Jacob. Together they **SAID**,"All Sock trolls will drop **DEAD**!"

P DEAD!!!

The trolls all gasped then held their **BREATH**, as Ketty pointed towards them the bottle of **DEATH**. "No little nugget don't give us the troll **BEGONE**,we won't cook you, so just run **ON**." "It's too late for **THAT**. If I were you, I would begin to **SCAT**!" Ketty opened the top, and flung it at the **TROLLS**. Some digged in the sand like they were **MOLES**!

The detergent got on their skin, as Ketty threw **MORE**. The sock trolls were slipping, trying to head for the **SHORE**. Ketty, Liyah, and Jacob ran towards the bags and grabbed the red **KEY**! They took the red bag with them, shouting, "Hurray, we're **FREE!**" With the key they opened the washer, which suddenly turned **ON**. "No!" Org cried but too late, the children were **GONE**! The team spun around and **AROUND**. They came out of the washer with a whooshing **SOUND**! After wringing out their clothes, they fixed their **EYES**. On something they've only seen in pictures, what a **SURPRISE**! They all eyes wide, shouted,"Oh **NO!**" they were standing in a street, in downtown **TOKYO**! Ketty frowned. "The washer took us to a place that even isn't our **CITY**." "how the others asked. "Oh don't you know," a voice said behind them. "What a **PITY**."

They looked behind them, and guess who they **SAW**? Org standing there waving his big scary **PAW**! "Not so fast nuggets, that was a neat little **TRICK**, but my skin didn't dissolve, it just made my body **SLICK**. Now give me my bag and I may end you **QUICK**!" "What this bag?" said Ketty with an innocent **SMILE**. "Hey Org if you let us pass it won't end up in the **G-FILE**." "The g-file?" Org repeated. "Yes the g-file Liyah said. "Yeah Org," Jacob offered. "For once use that brain in your **LUMP**. The g is where we'll throw it. In the garbage **DUMP**!"

Org let out a squeal, and towards them he **JUMPED**. He missed them each time, and Org was **STUMPED**. The other trolls tried grabbing them, it didn't **WORK**. "Missed us again," Ketty said with a **SMIRK**. They headed for another **MACHINE**. They jumped in, Jacob cried, "We got away **CLEAN**!"

Org came out, they dodged him left to right, like they we're doing a song and **DANCE**. They ran outside, saw the Eiffel Tower, they were in **FRANCE**! "This wild," Jacob said. "So cool," Liyah added. "Give me socks!" said a familiar **VOICE**. "No you big bully, we gave you a **CHOICE**."

YAAAAHK

"Oh really?" Org **GROWLED**. "Yahhhh!" the team **HOWLED**! And at that moment, they came through washer they again dried **OFF**. Jacob said, "My skin and clothes feel pleasantly **SOFT**."

Org came out, they dodged him left to right, like they we're doing a song and **DANCE**. They ran outside, saw the Eiffel Tower, they were in **FRANCE!**

"This wild," Jacob said. "So cool," Liyah added. "Give me socks!" said a familiar **VOICE**. "No you big bully, we gave you a **CHOICE**." So through the washers, they escaped, determined to WIN. To dozens of places they were in a **TAILSPIN**! They travelled to London, through Florida, even to **JAPAN**. Austrailia and Africa, They moved faster than **SUPERMAN**!

The trolls followed, from country, to nation, and from state to **STATE**. Org was out of breath and said, "This isn't going so **GREAT**!" All this travelling and running **ABOUT**, I Can't catch you guys, I am worn **OUT**!" He sat on the ground pouting, his head towards the **SKY**, and To the team's surprise, they saw a tear come from Org's **EYE**.

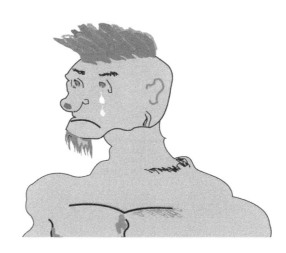

"Dude" Jacob said, "You're not about to **CRY**?" "No!" Org said angrily. "I'm...swatting away a **FLY**. This has been no fun," he said tugging on his wet **SWEATSHIRT**. "Without my socks everywhere I go, my feet are going to **HURT**! We don't have cars, nor buses, or **TRAINS**. We always go on foot, now our feet will feel **PAIN**!" Org and the sock trolls, sat on their **RUMPS**, scratching their toes, and rubbing their **BUMPS.** holding their faces, their sadness **GREAT**. Ketty looked at them, *really* looked at them, and realized she could **RELATE**. She looked at Org's feet, covered with scrapes and **SORES**. His socks were shredded from chasing them on a washing machine world **TOUR**!

The trolls with Org, together let out a big **SIGH**. All of them with big tears coming down each **EYE**. Ketty looked at Liyah and Jacob, they all should be **MAD**. Instead when they looked at the sock trolls, they just felt...**BAD**. Then the detectives rubbed their chins, and scratched their **HEADS**. They came up with a delightful plan and **SAID**. "Sock trolls," they **SAID**. "We have plan so you won't steal socks anymore, but make them **INSTEAD**. We'll use rolls of yarn and rolls of **THREAD**. With many colors including your favorite ORG, **RED**!"

The troll king's eyes grew wide. "Making socks? We don't know **HOW**. This skill we don't have, not ever, not **NOW**!" All the sock trolls at once begin to **GRUMBLE**. Looking at the children they began to **MUMBLE**. "Making socks?" What a waste of **TIME**. Stealing them is more fun, it's not that bad of a **CRIME**." Ketty gave them a hard **LOOK**, and said "Listen trolls its not cool to be a **CROOK**! Making socks may take time, but after awhile you will be a **PRO**, because we are going to teach you how to **SEW**." "Really?", Org asked. "You would do that for **US**, after all we did, you still show us **TRUST**?"

"ABSOLUTELY!" The children said. So the children each took ten sock trolls in a **CLASS**. Teaching with thread and needle, and the sock trolls learned **FAST**! They made warm socks for snow, cool socks for **HEAT**. Socks to walk on sand, and socks to walk on the **STREET**. Socks they could run in, socks to climb their favorite **TREES**, socks for games and for swimming in the **SEAS**. The socks that had colors of red, green, and **GOLD**. Grey and black, brown and blue, even the color of **MOLD**. (Org's favorite.) When the classes were finished, when the work was **DONE**.

The trolls cried with joy, "Boy that was **FUN**!" "Yeah it was!" cried Liyah. "No need to steal anymore," Jacob added. This made the sock trolls give smiles big and **WIDE**. Knowing they could make their own socks, filled them with **PRIDE**. "Thanks little nuggets for teaching your **CLASS**, we sock trolls really had a **BLAST**!" "We had fun too!" We are glad we could help, for you to learn this was really a **MUST**, but we do have one question, we're really going to eat **US**?" Org just laughed, "No we love to eat **KELP**. Ketty, Liyah Jacob, thanks for your **HELP**."

The team went back home, their mystery was solved with a happy **END**, Though scary at times a fun day together, they did **SPEND**! Liyah and Jacob told their mothers about the day they **HAD**. Ketty brought home all the missing socks that belonged to her **DAD**! (her Mom didn't like that) And every month the team a message to the Sock Trolls they'd **SEND**.

All glad that their foes were now called...Their **FRIENDS**.

THE **END**. Or is there more to **pen..!?!**

Lightning Source UK Ltd.
Milton Keynes UK
UKHW050628021219
354606UK00005B/64/P